SUMMER IN NANTUCKET

USA TODAY & WSJ BESTSELLING AUTHOR

SIOBHAN DAVIS

The Kennedy clan descends on Nantucket for a last-minute get-together that turns into a surprise family wedding. Catch up with all your favorite couples as they spend a few blissful weeks on the island, celebrating another special occasion, surrounded by loved ones.

Note From The Author

This is an optional novella in the Kennedy Boys series, and it should only be read AFTER *Forgiving Keven*. This novella takes place the summer after Faye and Kyler's wedding (basically one year later).

This book is dedicated to all the loyal Kennedy Boys readers. Thank you for loving this series and for patiently waiting for it to conclude.

There is no major drama or big plot twists in this novella. It's simply a light, feel-good summer read, designed to leave you with all kinds of warm and cozy feelings! It's a chance to catch up with everyone and share in one special couple's big day, and I wanted to give you some small, new insights into the Kennedy triplets as you waited for the final three books in the series. (Update – the series is now fully complete.)

My heart is seriously so full of love and joy after writing this! I LOVE this family so much, and I hope you enjoy reading *Summer in Nantucket* as much as I enjoyed writing it! Happy reading and thank you again for your continued support of this series. I'm writing these last few books for you!

SUMMER IN NANTUCKET

Chapter One
Kyler

"There they are!" Faye exclaims, pointing toward the door as Lana, Kal, and Hewson step foot into the terminal at Nantucket Memorial Airport.

"Aunty Faye!" Hewson screams, his little face alight with excitement as he bobs up and down on Kal's shoulders. It's been four months since we last saw them at Easter, shortly before his third birthday, and he's changed yet again. He's grown another few inches, and his babyish features have matured.

"Lemme down!" he yells, and Brad chuckles as Hewson squirms and wriggles on top of his dad's shoulders. Kal has a firm grip on his little legs, and a serious expression on his face, as he carefully bends down so he can jump off.

Faye abandons her suitcase, racing toward the little guy who captured her heart from the moment she first met him.

"I still can't believe you haven't knocked her up yet,"

Brad says, grinning. "Your brothers are pissed because no one won the bet."

When Faye and I got married last August, all my brothers—and Brad—made bets on how fast I'd impregnate my wife.

Assholes.

"I'm not getting my wife pregnant so my asshole brothers can win some stupid bet." I roll my eyes, smiling as I watch Faye scoop Hewson up into her arms, peppering his cute little face with kisses. "As much as we both adore our nephew, and we definitely want kids sooner than later, it won't be happening for a while."

"So, you're still planning on going traveling after you graduate?" Rachel asks, lifting the dress bag up so it doesn't trail the ground.

"Give me that, babe." Brad slings his backpack over his shoulder, reaching for the bag.

"It's fine. I've got it." I snigger as Rachel narrows her eyes in warning at my best friend. Those two are crazy in love, but they both like to be in control, which leads to a regular battle of wills. Rach gives as good as she gets, and it's funny watching McConaughey grovel.

"You are so stubborn." Brad shakes his head.

"You're only learning that now?" Kal says, grabbing me into a quick hug. He whips the bag out of Rachel's hands before she can protest. "No bitching or whining, Red," Kal says, in a nod to Brad's old nickname for his girl. "If anyone is carrying my bride's wedding dress, it'll be me."

"You shouldn't carry it," Faye says, attempting to hold onto a wriggling Hewson. "It's bad luck. Give it to Ky."

Lana smiles softly. "It's only bad luck if he sees it, and I don't buy into wedding superstition anyway."

"You are the most laid-back bride I've ever met, Lana," Rach says, kissing Lana on the cheek. "Most of the women I design dresses for put Mama Kennedy to shame in the Bridezilla stakes."

"Don't mention the war," Kal grumbles, grabbing hold of Hewson's hand before he runs off. He's a little livewire, and you need eyes on him all the time. I mess up his hair, winking as he gives me a thumbs-up.

We walk toward the exit en masse.

"I'm still terrified of Mom's reaction when she hears the news," Kal admits.

"Relax." I slap him on the back. "Once she hears this family get-together is actually your wedding, she'll be too excited to get mad."

"I hope you're right," Lana says, worrying her lip between her teeth. "Because I really don't want to upset her or have her thinking we did this deliberately to cut her out."

"Alex will be fine," Faye says, squeezing Lana's hand as we walk outside the small airport. "Like Ky said, she'll be too excited that you two are finally making it official to care."

"And you have a legit reason for doing it like this," Rach supplies. "You'll be too busy writing next summer to get married. It makes complete sense to do it now even if it was a bit of a rush job."

"I don't know what I would've done without both of you." Lana beams at Faye and Rachel. "I cannot thank you enough."

"You're family," Faye immediately replies, and a familiar lump clogs my throat. "And you're one of my best friends. I'd have been seriously pissed if you didn't confide in me."

Us four are the only ones who know about the surprise wedding. All along, Kal and Lana have been insistent they would marry after graduating UF, but Lana just secured a new three-book deal with a top five publisher, and they want the first manuscript by the end of next summer. There's no way Lana could deliver on that deadline during senior year of college if she was also planning a wedding, so they made the decision four weeks ago to get married this summer.

Kal and Lana love Nantucket, and they spend every summer here, so it didn't rouse suspicion when they organized for the full family to come out for a couple weeks. We've arrived a week before everyone else to help them put the final preparations in place.

"Sweet ride," Brad says, as we come to a halt in front of a long, sleek black SUV.

"I didn't know you owned a Lincoln Navigator," I admit, running my hand along the side in admiration.

"I had it delivered when we arrived last week."

"Something you want to share, little bro?" I inquire, arching a brow. I'm wondering if this new purchase might have anything to do with them extending their family.

"Lana is not pregnant, and this isn't a shotgun wedding," Kal says, lifting his son into the car seat and securely strapping him in. "Figured we could use a larger car with everyone arriving."

"It's gorgeous," Faye says, sliding into the middle seat

beside a smiley Hewson. "And it still has that new car smell." She inhales, closing her eyes momentarily, and an almost orgasmic expression appears on her face.

"I think your wife is turned on by my car," Kal whispers, waggling his brows. "I'll let you borrow it later if you want to get your kink on." He smirks, and Faye slaps his arm.

"Ky is the only one who turns me on, and why are you such a freak?"

Kal raises his palms. "Hey, I'm not the one who wants to make love to my car. Think carefully before you throw stones, cuz."

"I love it out here," Faye says, leaning over the wall at the back of Kal and Lana's one-story Spanish-style property, gazing longingly at the sea. The water is calm, shimmering eerily under the nighttime sky. "Maybe we should've bought a home here instead of the cabin."

I wrap my arms around her from behind. "I thought you loved the cabin." I sweep her hair to one side, running my nose along the column of her neck.

"I do," she pants, pressing her ass back into me. "I love the solitude and rugged beauty of Connecticut, but having a place like this, by the beach, would probably have made more sense. I know we're not planning on kids for a few years yet, but when they come along, we'll probably want to spend more time in Nantucket. Especially if Kal and Lana decide to stay permanently in Florida the rest of the year. This will be our only opportunity to hang out with them."

"We can buy a place here if you want." I came into the rest of my trust fund when I turned twenty-one, so money is not an issue. We have more than enough cash to last us a lifetime, so if my baby wants a place out here, she's getting it.

"And sell the cabin?" A whimper flies out of her mouth when my hand slips down the front of her top and into her left bra cup.

"Let's keep the cabin," I whisper, kneading her tit, my cock instantly hardening when her nipple stiffens under my fingers. "We already have plenty of good memories associated with it. And I like having a hideaway close by we can use during the winter months."

I surprised Faye with the cabin when we returned from our honeymoon last August, and it provided the perfect escape from Harvard on weekends. Brad and Rach have spent time with us there, and they've also used it by themselves. Kev and Cheryl have been holed up there this past weekend, availing themselves of all the amazing photo opportunities. I like having a place to call our own, and a place to offer family and friends too, but it's not really the kind of place you'd bring young children to.

"Are you groping me on purpose while having this conversation so I'll agree without arguing?" Her voice is drenched with desire, and she's pushing her tit into my hand the same time she thrusts her ass back into my hard-on.

"I never need an excuse to grope you, baby," I admit,

releasing the zipper on her jean shorts and sliding my hand into her panties. "You know I can't keep my hands off you."

"Ky." She moans loudly when I cup her pussy. "We can't do this here. What if someone comes out?"

"The risk of discovery only adds to the thrill," I whisper, nipping her earlobe as I slip my fingers inside her.

"You're so bad," she pants, shamelessly riding my hand. "But, also, so fucking good. Oh, fuck, Ky, yeah, just like that," she adds as I pump my fingers in and out of her hot, wet warmth. My cock is straining against the zipper of my shorts, and I need to be inside her right now.

She cries out when I remove my hands from her body, and I chuckle as I grab her hand, tugging her around the far side of the house, ensuring we're out of sight. I might have teased her about the thrill of discovery, but there's no way I want my brother or my best friend catching us fucking.

Pushing her up against the wall, I yank her shorts and panties down, spread her lips and dive in, licking her slit and plunging my tongue into her tight channel. My heart pounds in my chest, and my cock leaks precum as I devour her with my mouth and my tongue, and I could easily do this all day long, but I need to bury myself deep inside her, so I stand, quickly shedding my shorts and boxers, examining her flushed face as I slowly stroke my cock. I lean in and kiss her softly. "I love you, baby."

She wraps her arms around my neck, and a devilish glint appears in her eye. "I love you, too. Even if you have corrupted me."

I line my cock up to her entrance. "It doesn't take

much to corrupt you, Mrs. Kennedy." I thrust inside her in one fast move. "And you've corrupted me as much as I've corrupted you."

"Oh, God, Ky." She wraps her legs around my waist, grabbing handfuls of my ass, urging me in deeper and faster.

"Lean forward a little so you don't scrape your back," I say, in between thrusts, tightening my arms under her butt and supporting her weight.

"I need you in deeper, babe," she says over a moan. "And go faster."

She claws at my ass, and my cock jerks inside her. I pound into her, but I can't achieve the pace we both want and need in this position, so I pull out, placing her feet on the ground and urging her to turn around.

"Palms on the wall and ass in the air, baby." I slap her ass a couple times as she maneuvers into position, and then I slam into her from behind, shushing her when she cries out. I pump in and out, moving faster and harder, bracing one hand on her hip to help keep her in place. With my free hand, I tug the front of her shirt down and release her tits, kneading one at a time as I continue to fuck her hard.

She rams her ass back into me, and we have a good rhythm going when a familiar tingle starts in my balls, spreading upward. I move the hand at her hip to her clit and rub my fingers against her with urgency. Her breathing quickens, and she flexes her hips more urgently as I slam into her with increasing need. The tingle spreads up my spine, and I press down on her clit as my orgasm powers through me. She explodes on my cock, whimpering and pleading as we ride our climax together.

When we're both sated, I spin her around and haul her into my arms. She rests her head on my chest, circling her arms around my waist, and I know she's listening to my heartbeat because it's one of her favorite things to do. I run my hand up and down her back, pressing my nose into her hair and just savoring the feel of her pressed up against me.

I never take what we have for granted, and while I didn't think it was possible, I fall more and more in love with my wife every day.

She is my entire world, and I don't care who knows it.

"I love you, Kyler," she whispers, pressing her soft lips to my naked chest.

"I love you too, Faye." I kiss the top of her head. "More than anything or anyone else in this world."

She peers up at me, and my chest swells with the loving look in her eye. "I didn't think things could get any better between us, but this last year has been amazing." She straightens up, trailing her hands up my chest and around the nape of my neck. "I love being your wife, and I know I'm the envy of most girls on campus."

"I wouldn't know," I say, caressing her cheek. "Because I only ever have eyes for you."

Chapter Two
Rachel

"Oh, wow, Lana." A messy ball of emotion wedges in my throat as I inspect my friend twirling in front of the mirror in one of my creations. "You are absolutely stunning. And I'm so happy it fits."

When Lana called Faye to tell her about their wedding plans, we both flew down to Florida for a few days to work on designs and take measurements for her dress and Faye's.

Faye is matron of honor, and Ky is best man. They are the only official bridesmaid and groomsman at the ceremony, because Kal and Lana want to keep things low-key and informal. I don't think any of Ky's brothers will have an issue with it, but I'd be lying if I said I wasn't a little concerned over how Alex Kennedy will react to the news I made the dresses.

Alex created Faye's and Eva's wedding dresses last year, and I know how much she loved it. Initially, Faye had asked me to design her dress, but I could tell how badly Alex wanted to do it, so I willingly stepped aside although I did help her design and make the bridesmaid's dresses. I'm hoping she understands Lana's reasons for asking me this time and that she's not too upset.

"You look so beautiful," Faye agrees with tears pricking her eyes. "And it's so you."

"You don't think it's too plain?" Lana asks, biting down on her lip.

"There is nothing plain about that dress," Faye reassures her, and I nod.

The strapless dress is fitted around the bust, and then it flows in alternate layers down to her ankles. I used silk with a flimsy chiffon overlay and tiny little diamante beading on the fitted part over her chest, and it's both simple and elegant.

It's one of my best designs, and it's pure Lana.

It's also practical to suit the wedding. The actual ceremony will be held on the beach, and then the party will take place in a marquee being set up in the garden at the side of the house.

Part of the reason why they've decided to get married like this is to keep the prying eyes of the media away. While most of the furor over their relationship has died down by now, people have long memories, and the last thing anyone needs is nosy journos regurgitating the rape trial and Lana's false allegations.

"You look gorgeous too, Faye," Lana says, waving her hands in Faye's direction. "That color pink is fab on you."

"We're lucky we have the most talented up-and-coming designer for a best friend." Faye waggles her brows, grinning at me, as she runs her fingers over the front of her fuchsia-pink dress. It's got crisscrossing spaghetti straps, a sweetheart neckline, fitted top, and an A-line skirt that stops at the knee. It's really pretty and it hugs my friend's gorgeous curves beautifully. With her dark hair and tan skin, she's a knockout.

I roll my eyes. "That's more than a slight exaggeration," I admit, helping her get out of the dress.

"You have to get over that modesty, Rach," she says, as we both assist Lana in removing her dress. "You need to sell yourself loud and proud."

"I understand where you're coming from," Lana agrees, carefully stepping out of the dress. "I was the same when I released my first book, but I've learned how to market and sell myself without coming across as a desperate bitch."

Faye and I share a grin. "Lana, no one could ever accuse you of being a bitch," Faye loyally supplies.

I listen to their conversation as I step into the walk-in closet to hang up both dresses.

"Tons of people think I'm a bitch because of what I did to Kal." Lana is quick to correct her. "But I've learned to live with it. Kal has forgiven me, and so has his family and mine, and that's all I care about."

"I'm glad you've been able to put it behind you," I supply, walking out of the closet. "I know it can't have been easy. The media attention I garnered after all that stuff came out about my brother was intense, and it felt like I was living in a pressure cooker for a while, but at least it died down. I don't know how you cope with it constantly being brought up."

She shrugs as she removes her underwear and pulls

on her bikini. "I hate it, but it's not ever going away, so I made a decision to just accept it. It only stresses me out if I let it, and I choose not to."

Faye pulls Lana into an unexpected hug. "I'm so proud you're my friend and soon to be my sister-in-law. And not just for birthing the most amazing little human to grace the planet." Tears twinkle in Faye's eyes. "I'm proud of how you've dealt with all the media attention and so proud of your writing career. Having your first book hit the number one *New York Times* bestseller list is an amazing achievement."

"You've certainly set the bar high, Lana." I smile at her as I adjust my bikini in the mirror.

"You are snapping at my heels just as fast." She slicks some eight-hour cream over her lips.

"Have you started looking at properties in New York yet?" Faye asks as we leave the room and head to the beach to join Hewson and the guys.

I shake my head, adjusting the hat on my head. It's fucking roasting today, and the sun beats down on my pale Irish skin, heating it upon contact. "We're going to start looking when we return from Ireland." Brad and I are staying here for a week and a half after the wedding, with the rest of the gang, and then we're spending two weeks at home. We'll be staying with my dad, because I'm still not talking to Mum.

"I can't believe you guys are moving to New York after we graduate. We'll miss you so much." Faye's tone matches her sad expression.

We will miss them too. We spend so much time with Faye and Kyler, both individually and as couples, and I'd be lying if I claimed it wasn't a wrench moving away. But the job offer from Miranda Fanning is too brilliant an opportunity to pass up.

While my little side business is booming, and, to be honest, it's getting too much to manage around college, the chance to learn from one of the best in the business is almost too good to be true. I've no doubt the glowing reference Alex Kennedy supplied helped enormously, but Miranda seemed genuinely impressed with my designs and the way my business is scaling fast, and I'd like to think it's my talent that landed me one of the most sought-after jobs and not my connections to the ex-CEO of Kennedy Apparel.

"We'll miss you guys too, but New York isn't that far away." I try to reassure my best friend.

"And you'll be traveling the first year too," Lana adds.

"True, and I can't wait to go to Australia," Faye admits, opening the gate which leads down to the beach. "It's exciting to be only a year away from graduating, and I'm really looking forward to traveling, but I don't want any of us to lose touch. You all mean so much to me."

Her eyes tear up again, and I look at her funny. Faye is naturally emotional, but she seems even more emotional than usual.

"Why are you looking at me like that?" she asks, noticing my attention. "Do I have something on my face?" She rubs at her cheeks.

"Are you pregnant?" I blurt.

"What? No!" She shakes her head profusely. "Not that I'd be unhappy if it happened without planning, but I'm definitely not. I just finished my period yesterday."

"Ah, that's it. I was wondering why you were so teary."

"It's the wedding, and being here with everyone, and, yeah, probably a little to do with my hormones." She links her arm through mine. "I just love spending time with family and friends. It reminds me how lucky I am that I've managed to find this much joy in my life after losing my parents."

"I know what you mean," Lana agrees. "I loved growing up with the Kennedys, and when I was cut off, I felt so lonely even though my parents are fantastic. There's just something special when we're all together."

"Stop it, you guys." I nudge both of them. "You'll have me tearing up too, and I've a rep to maintain."

"Mommy!" Hewson's cute little voice rings out, bringing us out of our nostalgic moment. The little guy is barreling toward us as fast as his chubby legs will carry him, and it's a total cuteness overload.

Lana bends down, opening her arms, and he throws himself at her, instantly wrapping his legs around her waist. "Up," he demands, and Faye and I grin.

That little dude has every single adult wrapped around his finger. I can only imagine the women falling at his feet when he's older. He's definitely inherited the legendary Kennedy charm.

"C'mere, Red," Brad says, patting his lap. "I missed you."

I drop my bag on the sand and settle into his lap on the lounger. Kal runs off to join Lana and Hewson as they head a bit farther down the beach, sinking onto the sand to finish building a sandcastle. Faye naturally curls up in Ky's arms, and I share a knowing smile with my bestie. I thought they said sex gets boring after marriage, but if the sounds we heard from outside last night are any indication, that's bullshit. Those two are the most touchy-feely couple I've ever met, and they seriously can't get enough of one another. It's lovely to see, and I'm so happy for my best friend.

"Did you miss *me?*" Brad murmurs, nuzzling his nose into my neck.

"Honey, I was inside for an hour."

"I still missed you." He pouts, and I shake my head.

"What am I going to do with you?"

"I can think of plenty of things." His eyes darken, and he licks his delectable lips while grabbing hold of my ass and squeezing.

"Ahem." Ky clears his throat. "Do you mind not groping your girl in public. It's turning my stomach."

Brad flips Ky the bird. "Listening to you fuck your wife right outside our bedroom window last night turned my stomach, so suck it up."

I punch Brad in the gut as Faye's mouth hangs open. "Dickhead! We agreed we weren't going to mention that!"

Faye glares at Ky. "I told you we shouldn't have done that outside."

Ky wraps his arms around his wife, kissing her temple. "Don't mind McConaughey. Him and Rach are well acquainted with fucking outdoors in Nantucket." His tone is smug in the extreme.

"Asshole." Brad flips him the bird again. "I told you that in confidence."

I punch Brad in the stomach again, and he reaches up, grabbing hold of my wrists. "How many times do I have to tell you. No hitting, Red. It's not very ladylike."

I lean down and lick his mouth. "And how many times do I have to tell you I'm no lady."

Brad groans as I reposition myself on his lap so I'm straddling his hips. I feel him harden underneath me, and a surge of pride fills my chest. I love the power I have over him. How easily he gets aroused by me. And I'm the exact same. Sometimes, just one look from Brad is enough to drench my knickers.

"Eh, guys. Hewson's on his way over," Faye warns, and I swing my legs around and stand.

"Thanks for the heads-up." Brad stands, taking my hand as a naughty look washes over his face. "We're going for a swim."

"Wait!" I shout, trying to stop him as he hauls me across the hot sand. "I only just applied sun cream!"

"So?"

"So, I don't want to get wet yet."

Brad hauls me against his hot body. "Are you telling me if I slide my hand into your bikini bottoms that I won't find you fucking soaked for me?"

A rush of heat floods my core, and I narrow my eyes at him. "I am now. Dickhead."

He laughs. "Less of the dickhead, please."

I coined the nickname for him when I first met him because, well, he was a raging dickhead. But he's the sweetest man ever now even if he still pushes my buttons to no end. But that man would literally walk over hot coals for me, and I can't believe I got so lucky with him.

"Brad." I tug on his arm at the water's edge, halting his forward trajectory.

He hears the change in my tone, and his brow instantly creases. He pulls me into his arms. "What's wrong?"

I circle my arms around his neck. "Nothing, hon." I press my lips to his in a tender kiss. "I was just thinking about how lucky I am to have you in my life. I love you."

"Sweetheart." He winds his hands in my hair, kissing me more deeply. "I'm the lucky one. There's no doubt about it. And I love you to the fucking moon and back despite what I'm about to do to you."

"What?" I splutter.

"Don't be mad!" he yells, grabbing my legs and flinging me over his shoulder.

He races into the water like a madman, as if he's participating in a triathlon and he's got a time to beat. Water sprays up around us, sprinkling my legs, and I shriek as I pound my fists into his back in mock fury. Even though the water is warm this time of year, it's still a shock to the system, but that doesn't stop Brad McConaughey.

I gasp as he fully submerges both of us in the water in one fast dunking, clinging to him as he slides me down his body. I wrap my legs around his waist, and my arms go around his neck, as I mentally conjure up ways to get him back. He jumps up, breaching the surface, and I slap his shoulders, shrieking and cursing him out.

"You know your potty mouth turns me the fuck on," he says, in between bouts of laughter. He flexes his hips, drilling his hard-on into my pussy, and my core throbs with need. "You're so sexy when you're angry."

"Is that why you annoy the crap out of me so much?" I ask, pushing wet strands of hair out of my face and my eyes.

"It's called foreplay, Red." His hands slip into the back of my bikini bottoms as he walks us out farther into the sea.

"Only if you're sick and twisted," I joke.

"We're not sick and twisted." His expression turns more serious. "We're in love, and hot for one another, and I hope it never ends."

I wrap my legs more tightly around his waist, panting as he trails his fingers across my bare ass.

"Me too," I whisper. "I can't ever see myself with anyone else. I don't want to ever be with anyone else."

"Rach." He peers into my eyes, and I almost drown in the hypnotic depths of his gorgeous blue eyes.

"Yeah?" I drag my fingers through his blond hair, staring deep into his eyes, thrilled to find so much love shining back at me.

"You know I want to marry you one day, right?"

I shrug, a little shyly, which is most uncharacteristic of me, but this isn't something we've ever discussed so bluntly before. I used to think I'd never get married, but all that changed when I met Brad, and now that my friends are starting to get engaged and married, it's been on my mind, on rare occasions.

"Baby." He sets my feet on the seabed, holding me at the waist. He tilts my face up so he's staring right at me. "I love you, and I want to marry you and start a family, and the only reason I haven't proposed yet is because I want to be worthy of you when I do. I want to have a career and the means to take care of you and our kids."

I open my mouth to protest, but he quiets me with a carefully placed finger to my lips. "Don't, baby. Please, don't say it. I know you have enough money, and I understand you don't care about who owns the cash once we can provide for ourselves, but this is important to me. I was brought up believing the man was the provider, and I want to be that for you."

"Brad." I can hardly speak over the lump in my throat. "You provide for me in all the ways that count, but if this is important to you, then I won't argue." I cup his handsome face. "I want you to know I would love to marry you someday, but I'm in no rush. I love the life we share, and I'm going nowhere. I'm with you, every step of the way, no matter where life takes us."

His Adam's apple bobs in his throat, and his hands tighten on my hips. "Red." He presses his forehead to mine. "This is why you're the one."

"You're the one for me, too. The only one." I kiss him softly. "I also want you to know that I don't need a big flashy engagement ring or a big wedding. I'm not one of those girls who planned out her wedding as a little kid, and I'd abso-fucking-lutely hate a big wedding like Eva and Faye had. Don't get me wrong, I loved both their weddings, but it's not for me. What Kal and Lana are doing here is more my bag."

I kiss him again. "And I'm only telling you this so you don't go putting massive pressure on yourself." I gaze into his eyes, startled to find my eyes welling up. "I only need you to be there. Anyone else is a bonus but not necessary. You feel me?"

"I feel you, Red." His hands move to the front of my bikini bottoms this time. "I always feel you." He nips at my ear as he eases two fingers inside me. "And now my cock wants to feel your pussy hugging him. You game?" His eyes glint with dark, hidden promise.

"I like your devious mind," I admit, jumping up and wrapping my legs around his waist again, grateful we're far enough out not to be seen.

"I like your devious pussy," he retorts, pumping his fingers in and out of me faster.

"My pussy is not devious!" I protest, grinding my hips against his hand.

"Your pussy holds an inordinate amount of power over me, and that makes it devious in my book!" He waggles his brows suggestively.

"You're crazy," I say, laughing.

Brad shoves my panties aside and pushes his swim shorts down a little, freeing his bobbing cock. "Crazy about you," he whispers as he slams into me in one fast thrust. And those are the last words spoken in a while.

Chapter Three
Kaden

"Do you know what this trip is really about?" I ask Kev as we're seated across from one another on Dad's plane. My wife and his fiancée are in the bathroom changing my daughter Milly's diaper.

"What do you mean?" Kev asks, with a frown.

I roll my eyes. "You're so fucking pussy-whipped you've turned soft."

"Says the pot to the kettle." He arches a brow, challenging me to disagree.

"If your boss discovers you're losing your sharp instincts, he may rethink your promotion."

Kev, predictably, flips me the bird. "Don't be an ass. I'm starting my field agent training a couple weeks after we return from Nantucket." He leans forward, resting his elbows on his knees. "And what the fuck are you talking about? It's a family vacation. Like the countless other ones we've had."

"See." I prod my finger in his rock-hard chest. "Soft."

"Excuse me, Kaden." Cheryl pretends to pout as she drops into the seat beside her intended. "My Kev is a wall of solid, hard muscle. And I'm not just talking about the one in his pants."

Eva throws back her head laughing. "You won't be able to get away with saying stuff like that once Milly grows vulnerable little ears."

I hold my arms out. "Hand the precious cargo over," I demand, swooning when my daughter shoots me the biggest toothless smile.

"Now, who's soft," Kev mumbles under his breath, and Cheryl nudges him in the ribs.

"Do *not* criticize any man for staring adoringly at his daughter. I think it's sweet."

Kent makes a gagging sound behind us. "I think you're all soft in the head." His gaze bounces between all of us. "I am *never* getting married."

"Because you'll never find any girl brave enough to marry you," Keaton jokes, earning him a filthy look from Kent.

"I suppose I could just settle for the first girl who came along." He drills a smug look at Keaton, and no one misses his pointed dig. Melissa's cheeks turn red.

"Kent," I snap, jerking my head toward the back of the plane. "A word, please."

"Just drop it, Kade," Keaton says, pulling his girlfriend into his side.

"Kent." I eyeball him, and he climbs out of his seat with a shit-eating grin on his face. Eva takes Milly from me, and I follow Kent into the bedroom, closing the door behind me.

"What is your problem with Keaton and Melissa?" I ask, folding my arms across my chest.

"Who says I have a problem with them other than the fact both of them are settling."

"You don't know that."

He rolls his eyes. "I know more than you."

"So, enlighten me." I send him a challenging stare, prepared to wait him out. It takes all of ten seconds for him to explode.

"He barely touches her! What's with that? And she's only with him because I turned her down first."

That's news to me. "When?"

"At a party a couple weeks before she started dating Keaton."

"What happened?"

"She was all over me, begging me to 'make love' to her." He makes little air quotes with his fingers, and his tone is extremely scathing. "Said she'd been crushing on me since eighth grade."

"And you turned her down?" Because that's virtually unknown from the stories I've heard.

"Yeah, because inexperienced Mary Sue types have never interested me. And, I was semi-exclusive with this other chick at the time."

And that's also news to me. Not the inexperienced bit, because I know Kent prefers older girls. I've heard a few stories about MILFs, but I'd rather not know the details. Kent's manwhoring ways are legendary around Wellesley, and I've never known him to date or have a steady girlfriend.

"So what? It bothers you she went after your triplet instead?"

He scrubs a hand over his prickly jaw, and I notice he's added even more ink to his forearms. Bet Mom's thrilled about that. "Nah. I just wonder about her motives, sometimes."

"They've been together almost three years, Kent. I don't think anyone needs to question her motives at this stage."

"Maybe not, but I honestly don't see what he sees in her. She's boring as shit."

"Keaton isn't you, and he seems to enjoy her company."

"But that's it. They're more like friends than boyfriend and girlfriend."

"And that's your business, how?"

"It's my business if she's tricking my brother."

"He know she hit on you first?"

I nod. "Yeah, I told him at the start because I was suspicious of her, but he didn't care."

"Well, then, my point stands. Keaton knows the score, and he's still with her, so you need to back down and quit giving them shit. You know it'll just stress Mom out if you're bickering the whole vacation."

"Why is it that it's always blamed on me? I'm not the only one who causes trouble."

"I'm well aware," I deadpan, because Keanu is vying for pole position on the Kennedy Bad Boys list. Ever since he broke up with Selena, he's been gradually sinking lower and lower.

I clamp a hand on my brother's shoulder. "You're a

good brother, Kent, and I know you care even if you go out of your way to pretend you don't."

His eyes flash darkly, and he shoves my hand away. "Fuck off patronizing me, Kade. Go back to your pregnant wife. We're done." He storms out of the bedroom, leaving me scratching my head.

"Everything okay?" Eva asks as I settle into my seat again just as Dad pops out of the cockpit, telling us to prepare for takeoff.

Mom is already dozing with her chair reclined, and I watch as Dad smiles lovingly at her, pulling the blanket up higher on her body so she's not cold. It's not the first time I've noticed subtle little gestures between them, and I can't help wondering if something is going on with them.

They still haven't officially divorced despite being separated for years.

"Kade?" Eva grabs hold of my arm, glancing at me with a worried look on her face.

I briefly press my mouth to hers, closing my eyes as I savor the taste of her mouth.

"No sexing on the plane," Kent drawls from the seat behind, and I reluctantly break our kiss.

A minute ago, he was mad at me, and now he's back to cracking jokes at my expense. Sometimes, hell, most of the time, Kent gives me a severe case of emotional whiplash.

"We were kissing, Kent. I think you understand the difference."

He grins, winking at Eva before turning around and sitting down.

Eva smiles, and I know she secretly has a soft spot for Kent. She's one of the few people Kent talks to, and I've caught them deep in conversation a couple times, which surprised me. I didn't ask her what they were discussing, because I'm just glad there is someone he confides in, and if he thinks she's relaying everything to me, he might stop.

Out of all my brothers, I worry about Kent the most. There is something going on with him that I've never been able to put my finger on, and he dismisses my concern every time I ask so I eventually stopped asking.

"Is he okay?" Eva whispers, keeping one eye on Milly who is currently fast asleep in the bassinet attached to the side wall.

I sigh. "Who knows? He admitted some stuff, and then he got mad and stormed out. I've no clue what I said to piss him off."

"That boy feels things deeply," she whispers. "And I wish he would open up to one of you."

I arch a brow. "You know what's up with him?"

She shakes her head, and her hands automatically move to her belly. "I only know he's troubled, and I've encouraged him to talk to you, but I sense he's harboring a lot of pent-up anger." I watch as she trails her fingers over her little baby bump, and my heart swells to bursting point. Milly is only five months old, and we weren't planning on trying for another baby straightaway, but my super sperm had other ideas, and now, we're expecting another bundle of joy in six months.

I couldn't be happier.

"Mom has sent him to a bunch of shrinks over the years, but none of them have helped."

"I think Kent just needs to be loved," she murmurs, resting her head on my shoulder.

"He *is* loved," I protest. "And he could get any woman he wants, but he chooses to fuck around instead."

"Maybe he just needs to meet the one. Like I did." Eva runs her hands through my hair, smiling up at me like I hung the moon in the sky.

"There is nothing like the love of a good woman," I admit, capturing her lips in a tender kiss. "Have I told you I love you yet today?"

"You know you have," she says, laying her palm on my chest. "But even if you didn't, I'd still know. It's in every look, every touch, every action and gesture." She kisses me hard on the lips. "I love you so much, Kade."

"Love you too." I wrap my arms around her, holding her close.

Across from us, Keven has Cheryl bundled up in his arms in much the same fashion, and we exchange a loaded look. One that conveys what lucky bastards we are to have found two incredible women.

"I can't believe I slept the whole plane ride," Mom says, standing and stretching her arms out as she yawns.

"You were exhausted, love," Dad says, coming up behind her.

"Love?" Kev mouths at me, arching a brow.

"Haven't you noticed how much closer they seem lately?" I whisper as I grab the baby bag from the over-head cupboard.

"Can't say I have."

"You really suck for an FBI agent."

"Screw off, Kade. I've other priorities now."

"Man, I'm only teasing. I'm glad you've got something other than work and computers in your life. You were on the verge of becoming boring." I smirk, and he shoves me in the side.

"Asshole."

"Keven." Mom chastises him. "You better hold that tongue around Hewson."

"He lives with Kal, Mom," Kev retorts.

"Your brother is an amazing father," Mom loyally replies. "And he doesn't cuss in front of his son."

Loud laughter rings out around the plane. Mom's so fucking delusional.

"Only 'cause Lana muzzles him," Kent pipes up.

"And that goes for you too, Kent. And I expect you and your brother home every night." She points between him and Keanu.

"We're nineteen, Mom," Keanu says. "You can't demand that of us."

"I can when you're staying under my roof!" she shrieks, folding her arms across her chest, daring them to retaliate.

"Boys." Dad chimes in, placing his hand on Mom's shoulders. "We want this to be a relaxing family vacation. Just be respectful to your mother, all right?"

"I always respect, Mom," Keanu says, leaning in to kiss her on the cheek.

"I'm glad to hear it." Dad smiles at all of us. "C'mon. Let's go meet the others."

Kal and Ky are waiting outside for us, leaning against two black SUVs. Of course, Kev instantly gravitates toward the Lincoln Navigator, starting up a conversation with Kal on the pros and cons of the latest model.

Cheryl grins, shaking her head as she shares a conspiratorial look with my wife. The girls have grown super close this past year, and I'm delighted they get on so well. I've always been closest to Keven, and it's as if the years we weren't talking never happened. I'm glad we are back on track and that the women in our lives are good friends.

When Kev proposed to Cheryl at Christmas, I thought for sure they'd set a date soon, but they're in no rush.

Cheryl wants to wait until she has her photography business up and running, and Kev wants to settle into his new field agent job, before they even begin discussing a wedding.

They are rock solid though, so I get the lack of urgency.

Nothing could ever come between those two again.

"Earth to Kade." Eva clicks her fingers in my face. "You okay?" I glance over her head, noticing Milly has been strapped into the car seat while my mind meandered.

I tuck her under my arm, kissing the top of her head. "I'm perfect. It's going to be a great vacation."

"I know." Eva snuggles into my side. "I've been thinking maybe we should buy a place out here ourselves.

There's no way your parents' house will be big enough for everyone in years to come, and we're already expanding our family. As much as I adore your family, it'd be nice to have our own space too."

"I've already set up an appointment with the realtor in the morning." Her eyes pop wide. "I was going to surprise you."

She stretches up on tiptoes to kiss me. "You never fail to surprise me. And I love how we're always on the same wavelength."

"That's because we were always meant to be together." I help her up into the car before climbing in beside her.

Kent makes a gagging sound, but I ignore his immature ass, holding my wife close and staring at my beautiful daughter sleeping soundly, and think I must have done something right to have ended up with the perfect life.

Chapter Four
Faye

"I'm delighted for you both," Alex says, enveloping Lana and Kal in a mammoth hug in the middle of their living room. They've just broken the news, and I think everyone's breathing a little easier now she knows, because she isn't in the slightest bit upset. "I already consider you my daughter-in-law," she tells Lana, holding her hands. "But it'll be nice to make it official."

Alex spins around, facing the rest of us.

It's just as well Kal and Lana have a decent-sized house, with a well-proportioned living room, because the family is growing considerably, and it's like moving a small mountain every time we plan a get-together.

"I'm so blessed to have such amazing children, such beautiful daughters-in-law, and the most incredible grandchildren." She beams at Eva cradling a sleeping baby Milly in her arms before glancing down at her grandson. Hewson is currently clinging to her leg, while singing a nursery rhyme to himself, and he's the definition of adorable.

I swear, my heart is fit to explode whenever I'm in his presence. From the instant I met him, he's enchanted me. Maybe it's because he looks so much like Kal, and I see Ky in him too. Or it's because he's so full of personality and it's a joy to watch him grow up. Or it's the way his chubby little fingers clutch onto mine and how he beams up at me, with his cute, goofy smile, when I'm least expecting it, melting my heart into a puddle of goo. Or the way he snuggles into my side, with his soft hand on my stomach, listening attentively, when I'm reading him a bedside story. I could go on and on, because every interaction with him is life-altering, but whatever it is, the little dude has captivated me like no other little person ever has before.

"Are you okay, Mom?" Keaton asks, smiling at the tears pooling in Alex's eyes.

"I'm peachy, Keats. Just peachy. I'm surrounded by everyone I love, and we're in my favorite place watching two of my favorite people get married. Life doesn't get much better than this."

Ky snorts softly beside me, pressing his mouth to my ear. "If I didn't know better, I'd swear Mom is high right now."

"High on life," I whisper. "And at least she wasn't upset that we planned it without her."

"To say I'm surprised is a massive understatement," he quietly admits.

"She's happy for them, and that's all that matters," I surmise.

"Weddings always bring out strong emotions," James

is saying as we rejoin the conversation. "And you should be glad your mother is so demonstrative."

"There's demonstrative, and there's oversharing," Kent says.

"Or just plain embarrassing," Keanu agrees.

"I love that Mom cares so much. Don't ever change," Keaton says, crossing the room to hug Alex.

"You are such a fucking suck-up," Kent says, scoffing.

"Kent!" Alex shrieks. "There are little ears in the vicinity."

"It's okay. He's in his own little world." Kent showers his nephew with a genuine smile, but he's oblivious to the conversation surrounding him, still singing away to himself.

You know Hewson is a magical little dude when he's even managed to hook Kent in.

All his uncles adore him, and they're enamored with Milly too. There is something incredibly hot about guys swooning over babies and kids. Every interaction Ky has with his niece and nephew gets me right in the ovaries.

"That's not an excuse or a free pass to cuss whenever you feel like it," Kal says, pressing a kiss to Lana's temple. "If I can curb the urge, then so can you."

Kent mumbles something under his breath, deliberately low, so we can't hear him.

"This calls for a celebration," James pipes up. "I'm taking everyone out to dinner. Let's go."

"Are you sure everyone is okay with the plans?" Lana asks for the umpteenth time as we get ready in her room.

"Everyone loves the plans for tonight," I reassure her again. "And I know I speak for all the girls when I say no one wants to be hungover at the wedding tomorrow."

The last few days have flown by, and it's finally time for the hen and stag parties. Lana's parents arrived the day after Alex, James, and the rest of the Kennedys arrived, and they are babysitting Hewson together while we head out.

The guys are all sleeping at Chez Kennedy tonight while the girls are all staying here at Kal and Lana's place. It's one tradition Lana didn't oppose.

"Do I look okay?" Lana asks, turning to face me.

"You look beautiful." She's wearing a jade-green lace skater-style dress with black wedge heels and a pretty diamond necklace with matching bracelet. It's simple but elegant, and that sums Lana up perfectly. "And radiant, as every bride should be. Are you nervous?" I inquire, looping my arm through hers as we grab our purses and exit the bedroom.

"Not really although I'm sure I'll have butterflies in the morning."

"I kind of fell apart the morning of my wedding," I admit, remembering how my emotions were veering all over the place. "It really hit me that my parents weren't there to see me walk down the aisle, and the tears came out of nowhere."

She pats my arm in sympathy. "That's completely understandable, and a natural reaction."

"Ky was amazing." I smile through glassy eyes. "Not

that I'm surprised. He always knows the perfect thing to say or do at the right time."

"I don't think I've ever met two people more in tune with one another as you two." She squeezes my arm. "Don't get me wrong, I love Alex and James to the ends of the Earth, but they weren't always the greatest parents. Sometimes, I wonder how they managed to raise such amazing guys."

"Well, however it happened, I'm glad for it, because I couldn't imagine my life without Ky in it."

"To the beautiful bride!" Rachel says, leaning across the table in the restaurant with a full glass of champagne. We all raise our glasses, toasting Lana.

I'm not sure how the guys managed it, but we've had a limitless supply of alcohol all night with no questions asked. Even Melissa is indulging in a few glasses, and I'm hoping to get an opportunity to know her better.

Out of all the Kennedy women, she's the only one I'm not on close terms with. She's always very polite whenever we meet, but she's shy, and I think she feels like a bit of an outsider. She's a year younger than Keaton, which means she's a good few years younger than most of us, and until recently, she was still very much a kid. But she's starting Harvard soon, and she's all grown up now.

When Eva and Cheryl go to the bathroom, I seize the opportunity to sit beside Keaton's girlfriend. "Are you having a good time?"

"Yes. It's been great. Cheryl and Eva are really nice."

The girls insisted on putting Melissa in between them. No doubt because they knew me, Rach, and Lana would want to sit together.

Lana's bestie from college, Liv, and Kal's friend Brett's girlfriend, Tessa, are supposed to be joining us after dinner for a few drinks. They only arrived on the island earlier, and they're getting settled into their hotel before joining the party.

"They are two of the sweetest women," I agree.

An awkward silence descends for a few beats, and I clear my throat, grappling for something to say. I've never been great at small talk, and I don't know her well enough to naturally keep the conversation flowing. "So, are you looking forward to starting at Harvard?"

She smiles but it doesn't quite meet her eyes. "I am, but I always thought Keaton would be there too."

I shoot her a sympathetic look. "He took us all by surprise when he announced he was attending Berkeley. None of us had a clue." Keaton pulled a Kal—only admitting it at the last minute. Alex was inconsolable because California is so far away, and she's especially attached to Keaton, but he's made a big effort to come home once a month, and no one could ask for more than that.

"Neither did I. That's why we broke up for a while. I was so mad at him."

Keaton had confided they were taking a break, and I honestly didn't think they'd get back together, because doing the long-distance thing is hard, but they showed up at the house together last month for Sunday dinner, confirming they were giving it another go.

"I know he never meant to hurt you," I truthfully reply. "They have one of the best finance programs in the country, and I think Keaton needed an opportunity to discover who he is away from the glare of the spotlight in MA."

For reasons none of us understand, people are still obsessed with the Kennedys. Ky and I can't go out for dinner in the city without getting papped. It's one of the reasons I'm most looking forward to traveling. We get to be a normal couple, away from prying eyes, and there's a lot to be said for it.

"I understand that now, but it doesn't mean it's easy. He's so far away."

"And you didn't consider going there with him?"

The saddest look washes over her face, and I realize I've just put my foot in it. "Shit. I'm sorry, Melissa. Keaton didn't mention anything about that to me."

"I was willing to go there for him, but he doesn't want me changing my plans for him. At least that's one thing my parents agree with him on."

I place my hand over hers, because I can tell she's hurting. "I'm not really surprised to hear that because Keaton is the most selfless of all his brothers, my husband included. And he has the biggest heart. I know how much he cares for you and how much it hurt being separated from you."

Her eyes light up. "He told you that?"

Oh, fuck, fuck, fuck. "Not in so many words," I fudge. "But he was miserable as sin these past few months, and you've put a smile back on his face." Or at least she seems to be the reason for it.

"I know Kent thinks I don't love Keaton, but I really do."

My eyes pop wide. "Why would Kent think that?" I hold up a palm. "Stop that thought." I grin, rolling my eyes. "This is Kent we're talking about."

She smiles timidly at me. "They are all so different. The triplets."

"They are. I noticed that from the start."

Silence engulfs us again, and this time, Melissa is the one to break it. "I'm glad I got the chance to come here." She takes a sip of her champagne, smiling at me as Cheryl and Eva return to the table.

"We're glad you could be here too," I reassure her.

"Have we ordered dessert yet?" Eva asks, sliding into the seat on the other side of Melissa while Cheryl takes the seat across from us.

"I don't think so, but I couldn't eat another thing. I'm stuffed." I pat my flat stomach even though I feel almost pregnant after wolfing down a big starter and main.

"I'm eating for two," Eva says, grinning. "That's my excuse, and I'm sticking to it."

"I could eat dessert," Cheryl agrees. "Do you want to split one?"

"Deal," Eva says, laughing.

After the waitress takes our orders, the conversation turns to the guys.

"I hope they aren't planning to do anything nasty to Kal," Lana says, biting her lip.

I smother my laughter as I ask, "Nasty, as in?"

"Shave his eyebrows, his hair, or his pubes."

Melissa almost chokes on her wine.

"At least if they shave his pubes, no one will know," Rach teases.

"*I'll* know." Lana pins her with a look. "And I like my man hairy."

"Trust me, they won't touch his pubes," Cheryl says, her face pulling into a grimace. "And can we stop talking about Kal's pubes, because it's as gross as thinking about my brother's pubes." She visibly shivers, and we all laugh.

"They didn't prank Kade or Ky," Eva says, attempting to reassure Lana. "So, I'm sure you've nothing to worry about."

"Eh, only because I found out they were planning on tying Ky to a pole in the middle of town, naked, with only spray cream covering his cock," I admit.

"What the hell is spray cream?" Cheryl asks.

"She means whipped cream," Rach supplies.

"I'll add that to my list," Cheryl says, laughing as she drags her finger along the screen of her iPhone and starts typing. "Along with this week's other discoveries. Sun cream and arsehole." She giggles as she says arsehole, and it's a common reaction.

Melissa looks utterly confused, so I lean into her to explain. "Cheryl is keeping a list of Irish sayings for when she visits Ireland, so every time Rach and I say something she's never heard of, she takes a note of it."

"That's funny," Melissa says.

"I'll let you borrow it if you and Keaton ever go there," Cheryl promises.

"We should plan another family trip," Lana says. "I hate that I missed out on the last one."

"That trip was seriously nuts," I supply, remembering

how Kent almost got us all killed, on more than one occasion, and how my dad and James nearly came to blows over Alex. "Maybe you're all better off going alone."

"And you wonder why I'm worried about what the guys are up to." Lana sighs, pulling out her cell.

"What are you doing?" Rach asks.

"Calling Kal."

I reach across the table, whipping the phone right out of her hand. "That's against the rules, and I'm safe-keeping this for the rest of the night."

"You're mean." She mock pouts.

"And you're far too sober." Rach eyes her half-full glass suspiciously. "Give me her glass," she demands, and I hand it to her as she reaches for the bottle of champagne chilling in the ice bucket on our table.

"So much for not being hungover tomorrow," Lana says, giggling as she takes the drink and brings it to her lips.

Chapter Five
Keanu

"**W**ho's he talking to?" I ask Kent, watching Keaton flap his hands about as he talks animatedly into his cell.

"Who'd ya think." My brother snorts before he knocks back another shot. He'll be lucky if he can walk from the bar to the club at this rate. I'm trying to pace myself because Mom will lose her shit if we're all hungover at the wedding tomorrow.

"I thought there was a 'no calling the girls' ban in place."

"They're all fucking pussy-whipped," Kent says, shaking his head. "It's pathetic."

I say nothing, because the truth is, I wouldn't mind being pussy-whipped—if it was Selena doing the whipping.

And, yep, I've already got the pathetic part down pat.

It's over a year and a half since we broke up, and she still occupies real estate in my mind. I haven't seen her in person since last year when we bumped into her and that nerd Todd in Torment. But she's splashed across billboards all over Boston, and I've had a few near misses on modeling gigs in New York.

"I seriously don't get why he wants to tie himself down to her. She's as dull as dishwater." Kent swipes Ky's shot when he's not looking, downing it in one go. "I thought he'd finally come to his senses when he ditched her for California."

"Maybe he's realized what he had and lost."

I know I have.

But I don't have the option of getting my girl back because she broke it off with me, and she made it clear last year that she hasn't changed her mind.

"Ah, fuck." Kent peers into my eyes. "Don't do this tonight. Selena's gone, dude. Let it go." He shakes his head in exasperation. "You just need to get laid."

That's his solution to everything.

In some ways, I wish I could be like him. Screw my way through a ton of pretty girls without feeling anything. He's in it purely for the physical pleasure. But I just feel empty inside after some nameless, drunken encounter, and it doesn't help ease the ache in my chest.

There's only one girl who can repair the gaping hole in my heart, and she wants nothing to do with me anymore.

"Fuck this shit." Kent hops up, swaying unsteadily on his feet, following an agitated Keaton out of the bar.

"Sup, man?" Brad asks, sliding onto the stool Kent just vacated.

"Nothing much." I sip my beer slowly.

"You still modeling in New York?" he asks, and I nod.

"I'm usually there at least one weekend a month."

"It must be tough juggling Harvard and modeling gigs."

I shrug. "I'm constantly busy, but I prefer that." Too much free time means I think about *her*, and I'd rather fill every second so I avoid going there. Nighttime is a whole different ballgame though, and that's when the loneliness really hits home.

"Did Ky mention Rach and I are moving to New York after we graduate?"

I look up at my brother's best friend, nodding. "Mom mentioned Rachel was going to work with Miranda Fanning. That's fantastic. You must be proud of your girl."

A huge smile takes over his face. "I am so fucking proud of Red. She's so talented and so hardworking, and she deserves it."

"I'm considering starting a brand when I finish college," I admit, surprising myself, because I don't usually talk about this stuff.

"Yeah? Good for you, man." He chinks my bottle. "With your knowledge of the industry and your connections, I'm sure it'll be a massive success."

"It's either that or start my own modeling agency. I haven't quite decided."

"It's good to have plans and a few different options. You always were the quiet, intelligent one. And you're no stranger to hard work."

"Try telling that to my brothers." They slagged the shit out of me when I started modeling for Kennedy

Apparel at fifteen, but I'm the only one who has earned my own money from such a young age.

"Your brothers are proud of your success. They might not say it to your face, but it's the truth."

"*I'm* proud of my success," I honestly admit, and I'm not bragging. I've worked my butt off to become one of the top male models in the country.

I could've gone full time after I finished school, but I've never seen modeling as my endgame. I want to get my business degree and be my own boss. I like having a purpose and someplace to go to every day. Of course, in the early days, Sel was tied up so much in my goals, because I was the only guy she was comfortable modeling with, and we did hundreds of shoots together.

We had so many plans, and they all ended when she broke off our relationship. I don't just miss her in my personal life. My professional career hasn't given me as much joy now she's no longer a part of it. She's entangled in every part of my existence, which is why it's been so hard moving on.

"I hope you'll get in touch when you're in town," Brad continues. "I won't know many people, and it'd be good to see a friendly face."

"Sure. We can hang out. I can introduce you to a few people. It might be good for Rachel to mix in some of the same circles I do."

"That'd be great. I'm sure she'll be thrilled."

"What are you planning to do for work?" I ask, glancing over my shoulder at Kent and Keaton arguing in the doorway.

"You know I've been working part-time with Eva and

Kaden on their online golf business?" he asks, leaning his elbows on the table.

I bob my head. "Yeah, how's that going?"

"Great, actually. I enjoy the work, and they've just asked me to take on a new client liaison role when I move. I'll be visiting golf clubs and trying to bring more new courses onboard. It might mean some traveling out of state, at certain times, but I don't mind. Rach will be working a lot of late nights anyway, and we both like to be kept busy."

"That sounds awesome. Hope it all works out, and definitely look me up once you're there." I stand. "I better go referee." I gesture in Kent and Keaton's direction. "Catch you later, Brad."

I stride toward my brothers, ignoring the pretty redhead sitting at the corner table who's been eye-fucking me all night. "What the fuck is going on?" I ask, watching Kent shove Keaton.

"This pussy wants to bail," Kent snarls, reaching out to shove Keaton again, but I step in between them, forcing Kent back. "He's pissy 'cause he's had a fight with that boring bitch. Again."

"Don't talk about my girlfriend like that," Keaton says. "I know you don't like her, but that doesn't give you to right to talk shit about her."

"She's no good for you, man. You're either arguing or miserable. I know I'm no relationship expert," Kent says, and Keaton snorts. Kent glares at him. "But your girl is supposed to make you happy. Like the rest of the guys are with their girls." He jabs his finger in the direction of our table, and I spot Keven making his way toward us.

"It's none of your Goddamned business, Kent, and I'm sick of you sticking your nose into stuff that doesn't concern you."

"I'm just looking out for you!" Kent shouts, his nostrils flaring.

"Get the fuck outside," Keven says, grabbing Kent and gesturing with his head for us to follow him. "You're making a scene. This is your brother's bachelor party, and he deserves more fucking respect."

We quietly follow Kev outside. "What the hell is wrong with you three?"

"Don't bring me into this," I protest. "I only came over to calm things down."

"Great job, dude," Kent snaps, and I flip him the bird.

"Whatever your issues are, you need to resolve them once and for all," Kev says, eyeing Kent and Keaton. "Everyone is fed up with you two barking at one another all the time."

"You're one to talk," Kent says. "You and Kade didn't talk for ages."

"There was a legit reason for that, and it's not a good example to bring up, because we were idiots for letting it fester instead of talking through our issues. Be smarter than we were." He lets go of Kent, dragging a hand through his hair.

He's kept it longer since Cheryl came back on the scene, instead of the cropped look he was sporting for a few years, and it suits him better like this.

"You two need to sit down and get it all out on the table, but do us all a favor and wait until *after* the wedding," he adds. "Think you can be civil to one another until then?"

"I can," Keaton says, looking tired as he scrubs his hands over his face.

I'm expecting Kent to keep it going, but he backs down. "I will too."

Kev emits a relieved sigh. "Good." He grabs Kent into a headlock. "Let's get the others and head to the club."

They walk back inside, and I stay outside with Keaton. "You okay?"

He shrugs. Kent goes about things the wrong way, but his assessment isn't wrong. Still, I don't interfere. If Keaton wants to talk to me, he knows where I am. "I'm here anytime you want to talk," I say although he's heard me say it before.

"I know, dude." He stares off into the dark night, looking like he has the troubles of the world on his shoulder. "I wish I could tell you, but..."

I clamp my hand on his shoulder. "It's okay. I get it. Probably more than any of the others." I find it hard to share too. Not sure why. It's just the way I'm made. I look at my brothers, Kal and Ky in particular, and wish I could be more open, confront things head-on, but I just can't.

There was a time Keaton was an open book, but not so much anymore, and I know he has demons haunting him like I do.

"Do you think Kal would mind if I headed home?" he asks. "I'm not really feeling it."

"Don't leave, bro. Come to the club. Even if it's only for an hour. You'll feel like shit if you go home."

He considers it for a few seconds. "You're right. I'll come, and I don't want to disappoint Kal."

"It'll be fun," I lie. "C'mon."

"That pole looks sturdy," Ky says, as we amble down the road toward the only club on the island. He's swinging a length of rope between his hands, grinning wickedly as he eyes up the large pole at the side of the road.

"Dude, let it go." Kal chuckles, clearly misreading the situation. "You're not strapping me to that pole, or any other one, any time soon."

"Well, there's a challenge if I ever heard one," Kent says, sharing a devilish grin with Ky.

Kal's smirk fades a little as they stalk toward him. "Knock it off, assholes. Lana will string you up if you do anything to me."

"Even more reason," Kev says, pinning Kade with a knowing look as they join Ky and Kent, heading toward Kal.

"You should know better, dude," Kade says, laughing. "You were the king of pranks when we were growing up."

"We were fucking kids!" Kal protests, stepping back with an anxious look on his face. "And I'm getting married tomorrow!!"

"We know, and we want to ensure we mark the occasion properly," Ky says, exchanging looks with our other brothers.

"Were you in on this?" Keaton asks me.

I shake my head. "I'm guessing they planned this when we were outside."

"Nah, man. Ky has a rope. This was premeditated."

"Never mind Lana," Keats says. "Mom will lose her shit."

We both grin at the same time, running to catch up with the others.

"Fucking bastards!" Kal shouts, spinning around and sprinting away as we give chase. Brad is doubled over, laughing his ass off, while snapping pics as Kal ducks and dives, attempting to avoid capture.

But six on one are never good odds, and we overpower him in no time.

A few minutes later, he's strapped to a pole in only his boxers, and we stand around taking pics, enjoying his discomfort.

A few girls whoop and holler as they pass by, and Kal shoots daggers at us while we fall around the place laughing.

"You guys are going down," Kal says, fixing us all with a determined stare. "Consider this war."

Chapter Six
Lana

"Oh, Lana." Mom clasps one hand over her mouth, while taking mine in her other hand and squeezing gently. "You look so beautiful." Tears glisten in both our eyes as we look at my reflection in the mirror.

"I can't believe I'm here," I admit, moving my hips so the wispy chiffon layers of my wedding gown swirl around my lower body. "I can't believe I'm finally marrying the boy I've always loved in a gorgeous dress made for me by a friend." She squeezes my hand tighter, wiping away tears. "I used to daydream about this when I was a little girl," I readily admit, "but I never thought it would ever become my reality."

Her eyes shine with happy tears. "I'm thrilled for you, Lana, and you deserve all the happiness in the world." She pulls me into a hug, and I cling to her with an intensity that's new.

One chapter of my life closes today, while a new one begins.

I didn't expect to feel quite this emotional although Faye did warn me.

"Mommy!" Hewson screams, racing across the room as Faye rushes through the doorway, attempting to catch up to him.

My son doesn't understand the concept of walking, and I'm constantly yelling, "Walk, don't run!" after his retreating form. Not that he ever listens. He's a bundle of energy, wrapped up in an exuberant personality, and I don't ever want to clip his wings. But I do want to ensure he's safe, and charging around everywhere, with no fear and no limits, doesn't make it easy.

Especially when he has a father who likes to live life in the fast lane too.

I joke that it's like having two kids, but I wouldn't have it any other way. Kal is an amazing father. Even better than I thought he'd be, and the way he rains love on our son is a beautiful sight to behold. My heart tries to beat a path out of my chest every time I watch them together.

I bend down, opening my arms, almost losing my balance when he barrels into me.

"Woah! Careful there, little man," Faye says, reaching a hand out to steady me. "We don't want to knock Mommy over in her beautiful dress."

"I missed you, Mommy." Hewson wraps his chubby arms around my neck, and my heart floods with warmth.

"I missed you, too." I dot kisses all over his adorable little face because it's the truth. We are rarely apart from him, and it's almost like a physical wrench when we're separated. Hewson slept over in Alex and James's house last night, and I felt bereft without Kal snuggling beside me in bed and without Hewson jumping all over us at the crack of dawn, as usual. "So, so much." I tweak his nose, and he chuckles, and Faye and I share an emotional look.

My best friend is amazing with our son, and she's going to be such a natural mother. I understand the reasons why they are waiting, but I honestly think they'll cave and have kids sooner than later.

I can't wait for Hewson to have more cousins to play with.

"I slept with Daddy," he admits, puffing out his chest proudly.

"You did?" I'm not altogether surprised, but I wonder how much sleep Kal managed to grab with this little wriggler in his bed. I have never met any child as fidgety as Hewson. Even in sleep, he doesn't lie still.

"He was lonely without you, and he needed me to smuggle him," he says, and I giggle at his cute faux pas, straightening up before my dress wrinkles.

"Mommy!" He gasps, looking me up and down with his big, blue eyes. "You look like a fairy pwincess."

Tears pool in my eyes, and a lump clogs my throat. "Thank you, buddy." I cup his cheek. "That makes Mommy very happy."

Faye nudges Hewson, slipping him a box. He thrusts the box at me with no subtlety or pretense, and Faye and I share another look. "This is from me and Daddy. We love you."

I'm fighting to maintain control of my emotions as I take the box, leaning down to kiss Hewson's forehead. "Thank you, sweet boy." It's my turn to gasp as I open it to discover a beautiful heart-shaped emerald necklace with a row of tiny diamonds around the edge. It glistens and sparkles, almost dazzling me. Upon closer inspection, I note it's a match to the bracelet Kal gave me on my last birthday.

"Daddy said I was to help you put it on."

I kneel down, turning around so my back is facing him, grateful I've decided to wear my hair up. I was tempted to leave it loose and wavy, but if there's any kind of breeze on the beach it would've just blown hair all over my face during the ceremony, and I want nothing to distract me from the moment I've desired almost my entire life.

Faye helps Hewson with the clasp, and it's only once the emerald is resting on my chest that I notice the engraving on the back. It has mine and Kal's first names and today's date, just like the engraving on the inside of our wedding bands.

"Daddy said you're not to cry and ruin your makeup," Hewson adds, thrusting an envelope at me.

I move to the chaise longue at the window, patting the space beside me, and Hewson climbs up. I open the envelope and read the note from my soon-to-be husband.

Today I marry my soulmate. My queen. My lover. My best friend. My honeybun. Thank you for giving me a second chance, Lana. And thank you for gifting me with the best little dude any man could ask for. I can't wait to start the rest of our lives together. My mission in life is to love you and our children with every ounce of my being, and I intend to worship at your altar every day for as long as I shall live.

Love you, babe. Now and forever,
Yours, Stinky.

P.S. Don't be late because I may very well die if I've to wait another second longer to call you Mrs. Kennedy

"Why are you sad, Mommy?" Hewson asks in a quiet voice, looking up at me in confusion as tears roll unbidden down my face.

"These are happy tears, baby," I sob, overwhelmed with emotion, "because Daddy made Mommy very happy with his note and his necklace."

"When I grow up, I'm going to find my own fairy pwincess to marry and I'm gonna give her a sparkly necklace and a sad-happy letter just like my daddy." He cuddles into me. "I want to be just like my daddy."

"You already are, sweetheart," I say, kissing the top of his head. "And I'm the lucky girl who gets to spend every day with both of you."

"Ready, honey?" Dad says, threading his arm in mine.

"I'm more than ready, Dad." I smile at him, surprised I'm not feeling more nervous. There's a smattering of butterflies in my chest, but it's more from excitement.

"I've waited a lifetime for this moment, and I'm not waiting a second longer. Let's do this."

Faye brushes tears away, giving me a brief hug. She looks stunning in her bright pink dress, and her face is awash with emotion. "I love you, and you look stunning. Enjoy every single moment."

I start walking along the red carpet that extends from the back of the house all the way down to the rectangular decked area that has been erected on the beach for our ceremony.

I walk carefully down the path, clutching onto Dad's arm as the beautiful music the harpist is playing reaches my ears. Faye keeps a firm hold on Hewson's hand as she glances over her shoulder at me, sending me a conspiratorial wink. I grin back at her, excited for our surprise.

We step out onto the beach on the temporarily constructed walkway, which is also draped in red carpet with tiny white rose petals scattered on top.

The small congregation rises from their seats, turning to look at me, but my eyes are locked on Kal, and sobs block my throat as a sudden rush of emotion hits me out of nowhere.

He looks so handsome in his black Prada suit. He's sporting a thin layer of stubble on his chin and cheeks, and his hair is newly cut and styled artfully off his beautiful face. Even from here, I can see potent emotion radiating from his eyes, and I know he's feeling this the same way I am.

"Hit it, Rach!" Faye yells, thrusting her bouquet and the ring cushion Hewson's carrying at Keaton who is waiting at the end of the aisle.

The harpist stops playing as Rach presses the button on the sound system set up behind the makeshift altar.

Dad takes my bouquet and hands it to Keanu on the other side of the aisle. They both grin at me, and Keaton gives me a big thumbs-up, which helps me rein in my heaving emotions.

They are the only guys we let in on the secret—besides my father—because we wanted it to be a surprise. I told Hewson this morning that we were performing a surprise dance for Daddy, and he was jumping around the room with excitement.

Kal's confused frown transforms into a wide smile as Michael Buble's "I Believe in You" starts playing.

He proposed to me with it as a backdrop, and it's our first dance song for later during the reception, but I wanted to dance down the aisle to it, because it's come to mean so much to us. The words resonate deeply, and when I was editing *The Story of Us*, my first published book, which tells the story of our love, I listened to this song on repeat. So, it's only fitting that it's a big part of our special day.

Dad, Faye, and Hewson join me in a choreographed dance down the aisle as I sing the lyrics to my love while shimmying my hips and waving my arms around. Our family and friends smile, laugh, clap, and dance along with us as we pass by.

Liv reaches out, grasping my elbow briefly, and I grin at my college friend and her boyfriend Riley who have traveled all the way from Florida for the occasion. Kal's best friend, Brett, is seated beside them with his girlfriend, Tessa.

I can scarcely get the lyrics out, the closer we get to the altar, because my heart is so full it feels like it might implode.

"I believe in you," I sing when I step up onto the altar. Ky grins at me, accepting the ring cushion from Keaton as Faye passes Hewson into his arms.

Kal reels me into his embrace, forgoing tradition as he grips me tight at the waist before dipping me down low and kissing the hell out of me. I grab onto his shoulders, kissing him back with the same enthusiasm as our guests whoop and holler while the song continues playing in the background.

"I love you," Kal says, when he finally breaks our kiss, pulling us both upright.

I keep my arms locked around his neck. "I love you, too," I rasp, struggling to catch my breath.

"I thought you're supposed to kiss the bride *after* you've said your vows, but I'm only the minister. What do I know?" The man we hired to conduct the ceremony jokes with the crowd, shrugging his shoulders as he chuckles.

"We've always marched to our own beat," Kal cheekily replies, grinning, as he slings his arm around my shoulders, pulling me in close to his side.

"Daddy," Hewson shrieks, and we glance over our shoulders to where Kyler is struggling to hold our wriggling son in his arms. "Me want up!" He holds out his arms, and neither of us can deny his adorable little face.

"C'mere, buddy." Kal takes him from Kyler, holding him on one side while he places his other arm around my shoulder, keeping me close. I lean in and kiss him softly, loving how well he knows me and how much he loves and adores our son.

The minister beams at us, not in the least bit upset that we're rewriting the rules. "Are we ready to get this show on the road?" he asks.

"I've been ready my entire life to marry this woman," Kal says, earning a chorus of oohs and aahs from our female guests. "Let's do this, honeybun."

"After you, Stinky."

Chapter Seven
Kalvin

The day has been magical. Made all the more special because our son has been such an active part of it. It's after ten, and he's still up. Still rocking it out on the dance floor, reveling in the attention.

The little charmer.

We hired an official photographer for the day, because we didn't want to ask Cheryl and have her miss the occasion, but she's been snap-happy the last couple of hours, and I swear she must have hundreds of photos of Hewson by now.

"Hey, husband." Lana slides her arms around my waist from behind, resting her head on my shoulder.

"Hey, wifey." I haul her around to my front, holding her tight. "Saying that will never get old."

"Today has been amazing. You make me so happy, Kal." She palms my face, leaning in for a kiss.

"You make me happy too, babe." I wind my fingers through her hair, and I can hardly believe this exquisite beauty is my wife. I'm sure I'm mooning at her like a pussy, as I weave my fingers in and out of her hair, but I've zero fucks to give. She wore her hair up for the ceremony and the meal, but she removed all the clips after dinner, and now it's flowing down her back, just the way I like it.

Lana is effortlessly beautiful, and I love that she's not obsessed with her appearance. That's she confident in the gorgeous woman she is. "You look so incredibly beautiful. I can't believe I got this lucky."

"You haven't gotten lucky yet," she teases, copping a cheeky feel of my ass.

"You're a sure thing." I waggle my brows, blatantly slapping her ass, uncaring who sees.

She's my wife now.

They can deal with it.

"Oh, really. Hmm." Her eyes flash with mirth as she looks up at me. "I might have to do something about your arrogance."

"You wouldn't deny me on our wedding night." I subtly grind my hips into her pelvis. "Especially after we were apart last night."

"You're right, I wouldn't, but it's for me, not you. I'm horny as shit."

I arch a brow. Lana's a little minx in the bedroom, but I know her inside out, and she's hinting at something. "Is there something you're not telling me, baby?"

Her smile widens, and I swear her entire face glows. "I haven't given you your wedding present yet, dear husband."

I press my mouth to her ear. "You got something kinky, didn't you?" I pull her in tight, pressing my growing erection into her side. "Just the thought of it has me hard."

She giggles. "You have a one-track mind."

"You're only realizing that now?" I peck her lips. "I do, but only when it comes to you. Always you."

Her eyes fill up. "Fuck, Kal. You get me every time."

"I should hope so," I say, swaying us both to the music.

"And your note was perfect. You sure you don't want to write a romance book?!" she teases.

"I'll leave the book writing to the expert." I rub my nose against hers. "So, when do I get my present?" I ask, winking suggestively as impatience gets the better of me.

She rolls her eyes. "It's not what you're thinking."

"It's not?" I drill her with a knowing look.

"Well, it might turn into that," she agrees, grinning as she starts towing me out of the room. "If we can sneak away for more than five minutes."

"Give me a sec." I reluctantly release her hand, sprinting to where Ky and Brad are standing talking at the edge of the dance floor, watching their women.

The girls are in a circle, and Hewson is in the middle, impressing them with his rad dance moves.

Damn, my son's got game.

He's a total babe magnet.

And he's only three.

"Can you mind him for a few?" I ask Ky.

"What's in it for me?" Ky jokes, bringing his beer to his lips.

"Maybe I won't beat your ass for tying me to a fucking pole in my boxers."

"You fucking loved it. And all the girls passing by loved it," Brad says, smirking.

"My wife will not love it if she finds out, and I'd rather consummate my marriage than spend it on the couch."

"It's awesome, isn't it," Ky says, throwing me off guard.

"What?"

"Saying 'my wife.' I availed of every opportunity after we got married to say that. I swear I didn't call Faye Faye for at least a month after the wedding."

"That's cause you're a fucking pussy," I retort.

"Mock me now, ass face, but you'll be the same."

"Worse," Brad adds, nodding his head. "He'll be ten million times worse, and I hate to break it to you, buddy, but Lana already knows."

I arch a brow. "Who do I have to thank for that?" I'm already mentally elevating their name to the top of my shit list.

"We sent photos to the girls. Faye showed her, and she cracked up laughing, apparently," Ky admits.

I frown. Lana was terrified they were going to do something like this to me because she was afraid the pics would end up on the internet or something. I guess I should be grateful the guys let me keep my boxers on, and they set me free after a half hour, to avoid that happening.

It's the only reason I'm not planning my revenge.

"You're lucky she reacted well," I fake glare at them. "Fuckers." They laugh, and I jab my finger at them. "Just keep an eye on little Casanova."

"It's fine. We'll mind your kid while you're off banging your wife, but you owe me," Ky says.

I flip him the bird, as I walk away. "After last night, you owed me! Consider our debt cleared."

The instant we're inside our bedroom, I lock the door and slam Lana up against it, lifting the hem of her dress and sliding my hand up her bare leg. I nibble on her neck, moaning as my hand glides higher. "I missed you last night," I murmur, running my nose along the column of her neck.

"Kal," she pants, already squirming. "Wait a sec. I want to give you your present first."

"This is my present," I say, crouching down and shoving my head up underneath her dress.

Fuck. It's damn hot in here, but I'm a man on a mission so I don't complain.

I trail a finger along her slit through her lace panties, and she whimpers. My cock is aching as I bury my face in her crotch, kissing her through the barely there material.

"Kal." She rests her hands on my shoulders, over the dress. "You'll want to see this first. Trust me."

"The present can wait," I mumble, pushing her panties aside and swiping my tongue along her heated flesh, moaning as my cock strains against the zipper of my pants.

"Kalvin Edward Kennedy!" Lana yanks her dress up, eyeballing me with a serious expression that dares me to challenge her.

"I get so fucking turned on when you call me by my full name," I admit, stroking my palm along my hard length. "Baby, I need to be inside you. Right now." I grab her ankle, trailing my fingers up her leg again.

She sighs, sinking to her knees in front of me. "You make it so difficult to surprise you." She hands me an envelope, and her eyes tear up. "You're going to be a daddy again, Kal. I'm six weeks pregnant."

My hands drop to my sides, and my eyes pop wide. "What?" I splutter, completely shell-shocked.

"I only found out last week when I went to the doctor to get a new script for my pill. With the wedding planning, I hadn't realized I'd missed my period." She drags her lower lip between her teeth in a way I find completely sexy. "Say something."

I lift her into my arms, kissing her softly, before opening the envelope, staring at the scan photo of our baby. A messy ball of emotion builds at the back of my throat and tears prick my eyes. "It's real? We're having another baby?" Now I understand why she's been avoiding alcohol, and why she's not in the least bit hungover today. I'm guessing she found some creative ways to avoid drinking too much last night.

She nods, still looking concerned. "I know it wasn't planned, and it kinda messes things up, but—"

"But nothing, honeybun." I cup her beautiful face. "This is the best news ever. The best wedding gift ever." I slide one hand down to her flat stomach, keeping it there. "And I'll be with you every step of the way this time. You won't be doing this alone."

"I still hate that I deprived you of that with Hewson," she says, as a solitary tear leaks out of her eye.

"Don't, baby." I peck her lips, rubbing my thumb along her soft cheek. "That's water under the bridge now." A massive grin spreads across my mouth. "Hewson will be fucking delighted." Recently, he's started asking us why he doesn't have a brother or sister like all his friends in preschool.

"I'm glad we made the decision to move back to Wellesley now," Lana admits, "even if I am still worried about people's reactions."

"I won't let anyone hurt you, Lana." I know she's terrified that people are going to shun her because of her false accusation, but she pushed her concerns aside in favor of our son's needs, and I couldn't love her any more for it.

Being around family is what's best for Hewson, and I want him to grow up in the same environment we did.

I want to play ball with him in the park like Dad did with me. Take him fishing and swimming with my brothers like we did as kids. Spend summers in the pool and by the beach. Have picnics in the woods and so many other things we did when we were little.

I've missed my family, and I want Hewson to grow up surrounded by his cousins.

But I won't do it at Lana's expense.

If she's not happy, and she doesn't settle, we'll move.

It's as simple as that.

I pull Lana's head to my shoulder, wrapping my arms around her back. "Moving back home is the best thing for us, but if people can't get over themselves, we'll move to Connecticut."

We haven't told any of the fam we're moving back yet as we want to purchase a house before breaking the good news.

While Lana and I both love it in Florida, and we'll miss our friends and the gorgeous weather, there's nothing really tying us there. She's still estranged from her grandparents, and there's no sign of that changing any time soon. My in-laws live in Connecticut. My parents live in Massachusetts. And Lana's agent and publisher reside in New York, so moving back to Wellesley is the logical choice.

"And you're really pleased about the baby?" she asks, hesitation lingering in her tone.

"I told you I want a whole football field full of kids, and I like being a young dad. There is nothing to not like." I reposition her so she's straddling me. "I'm over the moon, babe. This is the absolute best news ever." I stand, holding her up while walking us over to the bed. "Now, unless you've got any other presents for me, let me demonstrate exactly how fucking ecstatic I am." I shoot her a wolfish grin as I roll her dress up to her waist, drag her panties down her legs, and resume what I'd barely started.

"Meh," Kent is saying as I rejoin some of my brothers at their table a half hour later. Lana is bringing Hewson around the marquee, letting him say goodnight to everyone before she puts him to bed. Once he's asleep, the babysitter will watch over him until my brother and his wife retire for the night. We're staying in a hotel suite down by the harbor, so Faye and Ky are rooming with the little tyke.

"What's meh?" I ask, swiping a cold beer from the ice bucket in the middle of the table and popping the cap.

"The foursome from last night," he flippantly says, as if we're discussing the weather or the latest episode of *Survivor*.

"I told you it was a bad idea," Keanu says, sulking over his beer. "Those sisters were stage ten clingers."

"The older sister had great tits, but those noises she was making were a real fucking turn-off," Kent says, because he's got zero filter and nothing is off-limits. "And the redhead just kept making googly eyes at you the whole time even when it was my turn to fuck her."

I shake my head, grinning, even if I'm glad that scene is behind me now. I've indulged in a few threesomes in my time but never with my brothers, and frankly, I find it a little weird, but whatever floats your boat. I'm not one to kink shame.

Keaton comes rushing into the room, from outside, his eyes all lit up like the Fourth of July. He slams his palms down on our table, and he talks really fast as he says, "You need to come outside! Right now! Quick!"

"What's wrong?" Ky asks, his eyes instantly scanning the room for Faye.

"She just left with Lana to put Hewson to bed," I say, reassuring him.

"Nothing's wrong. It's the opposite," Keaton

confirms, looking like he's about to burst. "Just trust me. Come on."

"I'll mind the table," Brad says, as Rach approaches, sliding onto his lap. I've no idea where Cheryl and Eva are. Possibly checking on Milly. And Melissa went to bed an hour ago, citing a headache.

Ky, Kent, Keanu, and I follow an excitable Keaton across the room and outside. "He's like Ronald McDonald on steroids," Kent grumbles to Keanu as Keaton practically skips across the garden.

"I fucking heard that, asshole," Keaton hollers over his shoulder.

Up ahead, I spy Kev and Kade leaning on the wall, their attention focused on something in the distance.

"What's going on?" Ky asks as we step up beside them.

"Look." Kade points at a couple down on the beach.

"Is that—" Keanu says.

"Mom and Dad," I finish for him.

"Holy shit!" Ky leans his elbows on the wall, looking closer.

I walk to Kade's side, and that messy lump is back in my throat again as I watch my parents. They have their arms wrapped around one another, and they're kissing, and there's nothing chaste about it.

"Does this mean they're getting back together?" Keaton asks, hope filtering through his tone.

"Maybe. Maybe not," Kade says, smiling broadly. "But I have noticed how much closer they seem, and Dad's called her love a few times now."

"I noticed that too," Ky says, "but I thought it was just a slip of the tongue."

"He's slipping her the tongue all right," Kent says, and we groan in unison.

"Don't be gross," Keaton says, nudging him in the ribs. "They're our parents."

We watch silently for another couple of minutes, and I'm not sure who starts it, but suddenly, we've all got our arms around one another, and we're sharing huge grins as we contemplate the idea that they might be getting back together.

It's something we've all wished for, but the more time they remained separated, the less likely it seemed.

"It's true what they say," Keaton whispers, after a few beats. "Weddings really do bring people together."

Chapter Eight
Faye

"**I** miss the little guy," I admit, as I sit forward in my lounger while Ky applies sun cream to my back. I don't know how the hell I'll cope without Hewson next year when we're traveling.

"I know. Me too." He presses a feather soft kiss to my shoulder, and I lean back against his warm, hard chest.

"Babe, you just rubbed your sunscreen all over me." He chuckles, pressing a kiss to the sensitive spot just under my ear, and a delectable shiver courses through me.

"I'll be rubbing it all over your dick next time if you keep doing that."

"If that's meant to stop me, it's an epic fail," he murmurs, nibbling on my ear as his fingers trek across my collarbone.

"Do you two ever keep your hands to yourselves?" Kent asks, and it's a timely reminder of time and place.

"Not if I can help it," Ky replies, reluctantly moving

his mouth away from my overheated skin. "My wife is fucking hot, and I want to touch her every minute of every day."

Kent makes a gagging sound while Keaton looks wistfully at us. Melissa went home a couple days ago, and he seems more relaxed now she's gone. I can't figure out their relationship at all, and Keats is uncharacteristically tight-lipped every time I ask him about her.

"I want to touch girls every minute of every day too," Kent says, shooting me a wolfish grin. "I just prefer variety."

"We've noticed," Kade says, eyeing him over the top of his sunglasses. Baby Milly is sound asleep in her stroller under a massive big umbrella, which is keeping her sheltered from the full glare of the sun.

"Aw, are you jealous, big bro, because you're tied to one pussy for life?"

Kade swats the back of his head, and I'm not surprised. He's unbelievably protective of Eva. "Talk about my wife like that again, and I'll give you a matching black eye."

Kent and Keanu have been partying up a storm since Kal, Lana, and Hewson left for their two-week honeymoon-slash-vacation around Europe. Two nights ago, they got into a fight with some local guys over their women. Apparently, the girls were flirting outrageously with my brothers-in-law in front of their men. Both guys protested their innocence loudly, but we're not buying it. Kent regularly gets into trouble, and he's rarely guilt free.

Their escapades have made for an entertaining week all the same.

We've been hanging out at Kal and Lana's place for the past week, sharing it with Rachel and Brad. We meet everyone at the beach in the mornings and tend to spend our afternoons poolside at one of the houses or enjoying some shopping or a late lunch in town. A couple of days we've gone biking, and the guys managed to squeeze in a round of golf on one of the days too.

This place is so idyllic, and it'll kill me to leave next week. After my conversation with Ky, I'm even more determined to put down roots here.

It turns out that Eva and Kade have the same idea, and they've just put an offer in on a gorgeous bungalow a half a mile from Alex and James's house.

According to Kal and Lana, one of their neighbors is planning on selling up within the next year, once they finish current renovations, and after being granted an informal tour of the property, we're already in love. We've told them we're interested, and we're hopeful that we can make a deal to secure the place before we leave for Australia next summer.

It's just us 'kids' here, at the moment, because John and Greta have gone to Martha's Vineyard with Alex and James for a few days, although they're due back tomorrow morning. I'm enjoying spending time with my brothers-in-law and their significant others. I love that everyone gets on so well and how effortless it is.

Life doesn't get much better than this.

I try to take a moment, every once in a while, to appreciate how truly blessed I am, because I have an amazing life, and I've so much to be grateful for.

We're staying here for another few days before

heading back to the mainland. We'll spend a couple of weeks at our vacation cabin in Connecticut and then a few days with all the Kennedys in Wellesley before it's time to return to Boston for our final year of college.

The summer has flown by, but I can't complain because it's been amazing, and I'm so fortunate I haven't had to work. It's great to be able to fully chill out before the intense pressure of senior year kicks in.

"You're all so fucking sensitive," Kent moans, shaking his head as he lies back down on his lounger.

"Speaking of sensitive," I say, swiveling around so I'm facing him. "You need to call my sister. She saw some of those pics you posted on Instagram, and she's really upset."

Kent bolts upright, shoving his sunglasses on top of his head so he can pin his full glare on me. "Please tell me why the fuck I need to explain myself to your sister?"

"Because you two are doing whatever it is you're doing." I don't have a label for what those two are to one another, and I doubt they do either, but they've been with each other on and off for years.

"I hate how I have to keep repeating myself," he fumes. "Whitney and I fuck whenever we see one another, but that's it. It's just casual sex whenever we happen to be in the same place."

"You know it's more than that," I plead on my sister's behalf.

"Not for me it isn't."

Anger starts bubbling in my veins. "Well, it is for her, and if you don't feel the same, maybe you should fucking end it before you completely crush her heart," I snap.

Ky squeezes my shoulder, and I know he doesn't want me to get involved, but it's hard to stay neutral when she's sobbing her heart out on the phone because she's seen the various photos he's posted of him kissing and mauling other girls.

"If Whitney can't handle it, she hasn't told me." He shrugs, like it's no biggie.

I hop up, incensed at his flippant attitude. "She can't handle it!" I scream, grateful we're on a private beach and the only other people around are a couple miles way and out of earshot. I hover over him, with my hands on my hips, blocking the sun. "You're not the one who has to listen to her crying her eyes out. If she means that little to you, just end it once and for all. Let her go unless you really are the cruel, heartless bastard you pretend to be."

Kent climbs to his feet, and I've never seen him so mad. "Fuck this. You don't know me. And I owe Whitney nothing. I have never promised her anything more than sex." His nostrils flare, and Ky yanks me back, pushing me behind his back.

"Back the fuck down," my husband says, his voice clipped, his body radiating tension.

"Why the fuck is this always my fault?!" Kent yells, waving his arms in the air. "I haven't done wrong by Whitney. I've told her time and time again that I'm with other girls. That what we have is nothing serious. I've asked her if she wants to end it, and she tells me she doesn't have feelings for me and she's happy to screw me whenever she sees me. And then I have to deal with this fucking shit from your wife all the time, and I'm. Fucking. Done."

"Calm yourself down," Ky says, and I'm surprised at how calm his voice is.

"You fucking calm down!" Kent shoves him, and this is quickly heading south.

Eva stands, walking around the back of the loungers to come up alongside Kent. "Let's go for a walk, Kent."

"No, Eva." He shucks off her arm as she reaches for him. "I'm sick of everyone blaming me for shit. Everyone automatically assumes I'm to blame, when it's not always my fault!" he yells, storming off, kicking sand up as he goes.

"I know you're not blaming him, Faye," Eva says in a soft voice. "That you're only being a concerned sister, and he'll realize that when he cools down." She glances at his retreating form, looking troubled. "He's a lot more sensitive than any of us realize," she adds, slanting us an apologetic look as she turns around and runs after him.

I sigh loudly. This is usually the way things end up going when the topic of Whitney and Kent arises.

"Whitney and Kent are a disaster irrespective of who's at fault," Kev says, butting into the conversation. "I'm not the first one to jump to Kent's defense usually, and I'm not picking sides or trying to cause trouble, but I've got to be honest, Faye. Your sister is the clingy one. She's always the one hanging off his every word. If Kent's at fault, maybe it's because he hasn't been forthright enough in pushing her away."

"And if he hasn't done that," Kade says. "It's probably because he doesn't want to upset *you*." He levels me with earnest eyes. "I hate that you're caught in the middle of this. That it's stressing you out. Because that's not fair."

"Ugh." I grab fistfuls of my hair in frustration. "Now I feel like shit for having a go at him."

"Maybe we can talk to him again when everyone's cooled down," Ky suggests.

"I think you two should back the fuck away and let them handle it," Kade adds.

"That's easy for you to say," Ky replies. "You're not the one on the receiving end of Whitney's calls."

I don't see Kent again until breakfast the following morning, and he's still avoiding me. Not that I can blame him. I've tried to put myself in his shoes, and he made some valid points yesterday. I've never seen him do or say anything which indicates there is anything serious between him and Whitney.

Kent doesn't get serious with girls, and while Whitney might think she's different, in my heart of hearts, I know she isn't. That thought pains me. And I feel for my sister, because I know she's hurting. But Kent hasn't done anything wrong, and it's not fair of me to level accusations at him.

Kent is blunt to a fault.

Sometimes, cringingly so.

Which is how I know he hasn't led her on. I'm sure he's been brutally honest with her, on more than one occasion, but she's not listening.

After we've eaten, I ask to talk to him out by the pool. "I'm sorry for upsetting you yesterday, and I'm sorry for accusing you of doing something wrong. It's just hard for me to listen to her crying and then see you going off with so many other girls."

"I'm sorry for overreacting, but the whole situation just fucks with my head," he admits, sitting at the edge of the pool, dangling his legs in the water.

I join him, enjoying the feel of the cool water lapping at my calves.

"Contrary to popular belief, I don't set out to upset women. I like women. I like sex. But I don't want a girlfriend."

"Why not?"

"I just don't want the commitment. I prefer uncomplicated, casual sex with no expectations."

"Or maybe you just haven't met the right girl."

He shrugs, and my eyes are drawn to the new tats on his arms. Both his lower arms are completely covered now. I'm not usually a fan of ink, but it suits Kent, and they are artfully done. "I don't spend time analyzing it," he says. "It is what it is, and I'm happy with my life."

I wonder if he truly is though. I'd love to ask him, but it might only descend into another row, and I'm trying to make amends for the last argument I caused.

"Well, Whitney isn't happy."

"I'm sorry to hear that, but it's not my fault. I'm always up front with her."

"I know."

He arches a brow, peering into my eyes. "You mean that?"

I nod. "I do. I believe you." My eyes drift out to the sea, and I watch the gentle waves rolling toward the shore as I contemplate how to phrase this. "Your relationship with Whitney—and it *is* a relationship," I add, before he objects, "is none of my business, but I'm asking you, as your sister-in-law, to end things properly with her. If you have any feelings for her at all, even if they are only fleeting, please consider doing the right thing."

His response surprises me hugely. "I already ended things with her last night. We had an hour-long FaceTime chat, and, before you say it, I let her down gently. I know there'll be occasions where we'll see one another, and I don't want it to be uncomfortable or awkward for anyone. She was upset, but she seemed to understand."

"Thank you."

"I didn't do it for you, Faye," he says, standing. "I did it for her, because the last thing I want to do is lead her on when there's no hope of anything developing between us."

"I get that, and I was thanking you for being considerate of her feelings." I scramble to my feet. "Are we good?"

"We're good." He grins, mock punching me in the upper arm. "You can go back to being your regular annoying self."

I mess up his hair. "Funny. And you should know to be careful what you wish for," I tease as I head back up toward the house.

James raps the back of his glass with a spoon, claiming our attention. Alex and James returned from Martha's

Vineyard this morning without John and Greta. Apparently, they were called back to work early, so they took a flight directly from the other island. Alex wasted no time demanding everyone attend a family barbeque tonight, and we're all on tenterhooks wondering if they're finally going to let the cat out of the bag.

I was beyond ecstatic when Ky told me how he and his brothers caught them kissing passionately on the beach the night of the wedding. They made a group decision not to say anything even though I know it's been killing them to find out.

I lock eyes with my husband as I grasp his hand under the table. A reverent hush has descended over proceedings and we all wait with bated breath for him to speak.

Alex stands, her face flushed and nervous as James reels her into his side, sliding his arm around her shoulder. "Your mother and I have some news."

Keaton can hardly contain himself. His foot is tapping anxiously off the floor, and he's seconds from exploding with excitement. My heart is pounding in anticipation, and I hope they make this quick.

The guys all share emotional looks. "Put us out of our misery, Dad," Kade pleads, circling his arms around Eva's tiny baby bump.

"We wanted to wait until later in the month when we were all together at the house to tell you, but we can't wait any longer. We'll call Lana and Kal in the morning and tell them."

"This is worse than going to the dentist," Kent grumbles. "And we already—" Kev slaps his hand over Kent's mouth, halting him before he blurts it out.

"Just tell us, Dad," Ky says, his voice choked with emotion.

"Your mom and I have decided to give our relationship another try. I'm moving back into the house when we return to Wellesley."

The table erupts in whoops and hollers, and congratulations are bandied about as we take turns hugging them. "I'm so happy for you both," I whisper to James as we embrace.

"Thank you, honey." He kisses my temple. "I'm so lucky Alex has forgiven me and decided to give me another chance. I'm determined not to fuck things up this time."

"Darling." Alex drapes her arm around James's neck. "We both did things that hurt one another, but it's in the past, and we're not going to speak of it again." She kisses him softly, and I clamp a hand over my chest, swooning. "I love you," she tells him.

"I love you, too." He pulls her into his arms, and tears roll freely down my face. If I was any happier, I would literally burst.

As if it was by prior agreement, all the girls, and Brad, step back, allowing them some family time. I clutch onto Cheryl's hand, and we share a smile.

Happy tears continue to leak from my eyes as I watch my husband and his brothers lock their arms around their parents in a group hug.

And there's one thing I know for sure—no one will be

forgetting this summer in Nantucket for a long time to come.

Releasing Keanu is the next book in the series. Available now and free to read in Kindle Unlimited.

Keanu

Selena played me.

Confirming I wasted years loving someone who didn't love me back.

It should be easy to move on, but since she dumped me, I can't shake her from my thoughts, no matter how hard I try.

Dates and random hookups don't help, because no one measures up to the girl I still love with my whole heart.

When she appears at my door, begging me for help, I can't turn her away. My protective instincts kick in, and I grasp this second chance with both hands.

This time, I'm determined to open her eyes.

To help her realize she made a mistake throwing what we had

away.

To prove our love is the real deal.

Selena

Keanu has it all wrong.

I let him go because I love him too much to continue holding him back.

And I've paid for it every day since.

I didn't think it was possible to miss someone this much, but my entire being aches for him in a way that isn't healthy.

It's why I continue to keep my distance even though it's killing me inside.

No one understands me the way he does, so, when my ugly past returns, threatening to undo years of progress, he's the first person I run to.

If anyone can keep me safe, it's the love of my life.

Maybe, this time, I'm strong enough to be the woman he deserves.

If my past doesn't take me from him first.

Available now in ebook, paperback, and audiobook.

I didn't believe my fractured heart and broken soul could endure any more pain. Until Jared rocks up to the art gallery where I work, with his fiancée in tow, and I'm drowning again.

Seeing him brings everything to the surface, so I flee. Placing distance between us again, I'm determined to put him behind me once and for all.

Then he reappears at my door, begging me for another chance.

I know I should turn him away.

Try telling that to my heart.

This angsty, new adult romance is a FREE full-length ebook, exclusively available to newsletter subscribers.

Type this link into your browser to claim your free copy:
https://bit.ly/TITMHFBB

OR

Scan this code to claim your free copy:

About the Author

Siobhan Davis is a *USA Today, Wall Street Journal,* and Amazon Top 5 bestselling romance author.
Siobhan writes emotionally intense stories with swoon-worthy romance, complex characters, and tons of unexpected plot twists and turns that will have you flipping the pages beyond bedtime! She has sold over 2 million books, and her titles are translated into several languages.

Prior to becoming a full-time writer, Siobhan forged a successful corporate career in human resource management.

She lives in the Garden County of Ireland with her husband and two sons.

You can connect with Siobhan in the following ways:

Website: www.siobhandavis.com
Facebook: AuthorSiobhanDavis
Instagram: @siobhandavisauthor
Tiktok: @siobhandavisauthor
Email: siobhan@siobhandavis.com

Books by Siobhan Davis

KENNEDY BOYS SERIES
Upper Young Adult/New Adult Contemporary Romance

Finding Kyler
Losing Kyler
Keeping Kyler
The Irish Getaway
Loving Kalvin
Saving Brad
Seducing Kaden
Forgiving Keven
Summer in Nantucket
Releasing Keanu
Adoring Keaton
Reforming Kent
Moonlight in Massachusetts

STAND-ALONES
New Adult Contemporary Romance

Inseparable
Incognito
When Forever Changes

No Feelings Involved
Still Falling for You
Second Chances Box Set
Holding on to Forever
Always Meant to Be
Tell It to My Heart
The One I Want

Reverse Harem Romance

Surviving Amber Springs

Dark Mafia Romance

Vengeance of a Mafia Queen

RYDEVILLE ELITE SERIES

Dark High School Romance

Cruel Intentions
Twisted Betrayal
Sweet Retribution
Charlie
Jackson
Sawyer
*The Hate I Feel^*
*Drew^*

MAZZONE MAFIA SERIES
Dark Mafia Romance

Condemned to Love
Forbidden to Love
Scared to Love
Mazzone Mafia: The Complete Series

THE ACCARDI TWINS
Dark Mafia Romance

*CKONY #1^*
*CKONY #2^*

THE SAINTHOOD (BOYS OF LOWELL HIGH)
Dark HS Reverse Harem Romance

Resurrection
Rebellion
Reign
Revere
The Sainthood: The Complete Series

DIRTY CRAZY BAD DUET

Dark College Reverse Harem Romance

Dirty Crazy Bad - A Prequel Short Story
Dirty Crazy Bad # 1
Dirty Crazy Bad #2

ALL OF ME DUET

Angsty New Adult Romance

Say I'm The One
Let Me Love You
Hold Me Close
*Reeve**
All of Me: The Complete Series

ALINTHIA SERIES

Upper YA/NA Paranormal Romance/Reverse Harem

The Lost Savior
The Secret Heir
The Warrior Princess
The Chosen One
*The Rightful Queen^*

SAVEN SERIES

Young Adult Science Fiction/Paranormal Romance

Saven Deception
Logan
Saven Disclosure
Saven Denial
Saven Defiance
Axton
Saven Deliverance
Saven: The Complete Series

^Release date to be confirmed

* Coming 2023